Dear Parents and Educators,

Welcome to Penguin Young Readers! As parents and educators, you know that each child develops at his or her own pace—in terms of speech, critical thinking, and, of course, reading. Penguin Young Readers recognizes this fact. As a result, each Penguin Young Readers book is assigned a traditional easy-to-read level (1–4) as well as a Guided Reading Level (A–P). Both of these systems will help you choose the right book for your child. Please refer to the back of each book for specific leveling information. Penguin Young Readers features esteemed authors and illustrators, stories about favorite characters, fascinating nonfiction, and more!

Three by the Sea

LEVEL 3

GUIDED READING LEVEL **J**

This book is perfect for a **Transitional Reader** who:
- can read multisyllable and compound words;
- can read words with prefixes and suffixes;
- is able to identify story elements (beginning, middle, end, plot, setting, characters, problem, solution); and
- can understand different points of view.

Here are some **activities** you can do during and after reading this book:
- Reading with Expression: Although many transitional readers can read text accurately, they may read slowly or not smoothly and pay little or no attention to punctuation. One way to improve this is to read out loud with the child. For example, read pages 44 and 45 in this story out loud. Ask the child to pay special attention to how your voice changes when you read the word *them* and when you come to different types of punctuation, such as the periods, exclamation points, and ellipses. Then have the child read another page out loud to you.
- Creative Writing: Lolly, Spider, and Sam each tell a story that has a rat and a cat as characters. On a separate sheet of paper, work with the child to write another story with these same characters.

Remember, sharing the love of reading with a child is the best gift you can give!

—Bonnie Bader, EdM
  Penguin Young Readers program

*Penguin Young Readers are leveled by independent reviewers applying the standards developed by Irene Fountas and Gay Su Pinnell in *Matching Books to Readers: Using Leveled Books in Guided Reading*, Heinemann, 1999.

For Paula Danziger—EM

.

Penguin Young Readers
Published by the Penguin Group
Penguin Group (USA) Inc., 375 Hudson Street, New York, New York 10014, USA
Penguin Group (Canada), 90 Eglinton Avenue East, Suite 700, Toronto, Ontario M4P 2Y3, Canada
(a division of Pearson Penguin Canada Inc.)
Penguin Books Ltd., 80 Strand, London WC2R 0RL, England
Penguin Group Ireland, 25 St. Stephen's Green, Dublin 2, Ireland (a division of Penguin Books Ltd.)
Penguin Group (Australia), 250 Camberwell Road, Camberwell, Victoria 3124, Australia
(a division of Pearson Australia Group Pty. Ltd.)
Penguin Books India Pvt. Ltd., 11 Community Centre, Panchsheel Park, New Delhi—110 017, India
Penguin Group (NZ), 67 Apollo Drive, Rosedale, Auckland 0632, New Zealand
(a division of Pearson New Zealand Ltd.)
Penguin Books (South Africa) (Pty.) Ltd., 24 Sturdee Avenue,
Rosebank, Johannesburg 2196, South Africa

Penguin Books Ltd., Registered Offices: 80 Strand, London WC2R 0RL, England

Text copyright © 1981 by Edward Marshall. Illustrations copyright © 1981 by James Marshall. All rights reserved. First published in 1981 by Dial Books for Young Readers, an imprint of Penguin Group (USA) Inc. Published in a Puffin Easy-to-Read edition in 1994. Published in 2012 by Penguin Young Readers, an imprint of Penguin Group (USA) Inc., 345 Hudson Street, New York, New York 10014. Manufactured in China.

The Library of Congress has catalogued the Dial edition under
the following Control Number: 80026097

ISBN 978-0-14-037004-1   10 9 8 7 6 5 4 3 2 1

THREE
BY THE SEA

by Edward Marshall
pictures by James Marshall

Penguin Young Readers
An Imprint of Penguin Group (USA) Inc.

A Picnic

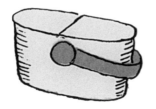

Lolly, Spider, and Sam

had a picnic on the beach.

"I'm as full as a tick," said Lolly.

"Me too," said Sam.

"Hot dogs and lemonade

always hit the spot."

"Now for a swim," said Spider.

"Oh no," said Lolly.

"Not so soon after lunch."

"Rats," said Spider.

"How about a nap?" asked Sam.

"Oh no," said the others.

"Naps are no fun at all."

"Very true," said Sam.

"Want to hear a story?" asked Lolly.

"I brought along my reader."

"A fine idea," said her friends.

"Then let's begin," said Lolly.

Lolly's Story

The rat saw the cat and the dog.

"I see them," said the rat.

"I see the cat and the dog."

The dog and the cat saw the rat.

"We see the rat," they said.

And that was that.

"Is *that* the story?" said Sam.

"Is that *all*?" said Spider.

"That's it," said Lolly.

"I didn't like it one bit," said Sam.

"Dull," said Spider.

"I can tell a better story
than that!" said Sam.

"I bet you can't!" said Lolly.

"Can!" said Sam.

"Let him try," said Spider.

"Okay," said Lolly.

"But it has to be about
a rat and a cat."

"Easy," said Sam.

"Sit down."

Lolly and Spider sat down.

And Sam began his story.

"A rat went for a walk," said Sam.

"So what?" said Lolly.

"Let Sam finish his story,"
said Spider.

"Thank you," said Sam.

Sam's Story

A rat went for a walk.

"What a fine day," he said.

"The sun is shining

and all is well."

Soon he came to a shop.

"My, my," said the rat.

"What a pretty cat.

And I have never had a cat."

"I will buy that cat and
have a friend," he said.

And he went into the shop.
"I want a cat," he said.

"Are you sure you want a *cat*?"

asked the owner.

"I am sure," said the rat.

"And I want that one."

"That will be ten cents,"
said the man.
"If you are *sure*."

"I am sure," said the rat.
"Here is my last dime.
Give me my cat."

The rat and the cat left the shop.

"We will be friends," said the rat.

"Do you think so?" said the cat.

"Well, we'll see."

The rat and the cat sat in the sun.

"What do you do for fun?"

asked the rat.

"I like to catch things," said the cat.

"That's nice," said the rat.

"I am hungry," said the cat.

"How about lunch?"

"A fine idea," said the rat.

"What is your favorite dish?"

"I do not want to say," said the cat.

"You can tell me," said the rat.

"We are friends."

"Are you *sure* you want to know?"

said the cat.

"I am sure," said the rat.

"Tell me what you like to eat."

"I will tell you," said the cat.
"But let us go where we can
be alone."

"Fine with me," said the rat.

The cat and the rat
went to the beach.

"I know," said the rat.
"Fish.
You like to eat fish."

"Not at all," said the cat.

"It's much better than fish."

"Tell me," said the rat.

"I just *have* to know."

"Come closer," said the cat.

"And I will tell you."

"Yes?" said the rat.

"What I like," said the cat, "is . . .

. . . CHEESE! I love cheese!"

"So do I," said the rat.

"And I have some here."

"Hooray!" said the cat.

"And now we are friends."

So they sat on the beach

and ate the cheese.

And that was that.

"Very sweet," said Lolly.

Spider looked cross.

"I did not like the end," he said.

"It was dumb."

"Then *you* tell a story,"

said Sam.

"Easy as pie," said Spider.

"And I'll make it *scary*, too."

Spider's Story

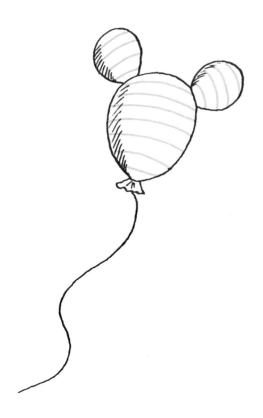

One day a monster came
out of the sea.

He had big yellow eyes.

He had sharp green teeth.

He had long black claws.

And he was really mean.

It was time for lunch,

and he was hungry.

On the beach he saw some cheese.

"Blah!" he said.

"I hate cheese."

And he went on by.

Soon he came to a rat.

The rat did not hear him.

He was asleep.

"Too small," said the monster.

And he went on by.

Down the beach he came upon a cat.

But monsters don't eat cats.

So he went on by.

Monsters really like kids.

On toast!

"There must be some tasty kids
on this beach," he said.

Very soon he saw some.

"Yum!" he said.

"Two boys and a girl!

Nice and juicy!

I'll have *them* for lunch!

But if they see me,

they will run away."

So the monster was very quiet.

He tiptoed up behind the kids.

They did not hear him.

They were telling stories.

He crept closer . . .

and closer . . .

"Look out!" cried Spider.

Lolly and Sam jumped 10 feet.

"Help!" they cried.

"He's going to eat us!"

But there was no monster.

No monster at all.

Spider laughed himself silly.

"Did you like it?" he asked.

"Oh yes," said Lolly and Sam.

"But we were not scared a *bit*."

"How about a swim?" said Spider.

"That's a fine idea!"

said his friends.

And that was that.